This Bing book belongs to:

....

Bing™ Annual 2022

Copyright © 2021 Acamar Films Ltd
The *Bing* television series is created by Acamar Films and Brown Bag Films and adapted from the original books by Ted Dewan.

Hula Hoop (pp.10–17) is based on the original story by Sascha Paladino, Philip Bergkvist, Lucy Murphy, Mikael Shields and Ted Dewan.
House (pp.30–37) is based on the original story written by Chris Parker, Lucy Murphy, Mikael Shields and Ted Dewan.
Stuck (pp.50–57) is based on the original story written by Samantha Hill, Lucy Murphy, Mikael Shields and An Vrombaut.

Published in Great Britain by HarperCollins *Children's Books* in 2021
HarperCollins *Children's Books* is a division of HarperCollins*Publishers* Ltd
1 London Bridge Street, London SE1 9GF

www.harpercollins.co.uk

HarperCollins*Publishers*, 1st Floor, Watermarque Building
Ringsend Road, Dublin 4, Ireland

Written by Lauren Holowaty

P26 Shutterstock 492944986 by kelttt

1 3 5 7 9 10 8 6 4 2
ISBN: 978-0-00-846785-2
Printed in Italy by Rotolito

MIX
Paper from
responsible sources
FSC™
www.fsc.org
FSC® C007454

FSC™ is a non-profit international organisation established to promote the responsible management of the world's forests. Products carrying the FSC label are independently certified to assure consumers that they come from forests that are managed to meet the social, economic and ecological needs of present and future generations, and other controlled sources.

Find out more about HarperCollins and the environment at
www.harpercollins.co.uk/green

ACAMARFILMS

Contents

Christmas colouring

Bing and his friends are getting ready for Christmas. They are very **excited!** Use your **favourite** pencils or crayons to colour in their pictures and trace over their names.

Bing has a special present for Flop.

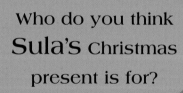

Who do you think **Sula's** Christmas present is for?

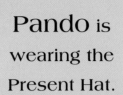

Pando is wearing the Present Hat.

Pando

Nicky loves Christmas!

Nicky

Are you excited about Christmas too?

Present match

Bing loves giving **presents** to his friends. Can you match each toy to the wrapped present? Use your finger or a pencil to **draw lines** connecting each pair.

Decorate the Christmas tree!

Can you help Bing, Sula, Flop and Amma finish **decorating** the Christmas tree using your favourite colouring pencils?

Hula Hoop

Round the corner, not far away,
Bing learns something new today!

Choo-choo! Choo-choo!

Bing is playing with his train when
Coco and Charlie arrive.
"Hi, Bing!" Coco says. "Look what I've got!"

Bing points to the big hoop
she's holding and asks,
"What's that?"
"It's Holly Hula Hoop,"
explains Coco. "I can do *lots*
of hulas with her."

Coco puts the Hula Hoop over her head and spins it
around her waist,

"Hu-la, hu-la, hu-la!" she giggles.

Bing's eyes open wide.
Holly Hula Hoop looks
lots of fun!
"Hmm, that was three
hulas," says Coco, "but
I did *seven* at home."

Bing *really* wants to try Holly Hula.
"Can I do it?" he asks.
"Yes," says Coco. "I'll show
you how."

Coco puts the hoop around her waist.
"You stand like this... then you spin the
hoop and do this!" Coco sways her hips
back and forth, saying,

"Hu-la, hu-la!"

Bing and Flop move
their hips like Coco
and say, "Hu-la, hu-la!"

*Clatter,
clatter*

Holly Hula Hoop falls to the ground.
"Me now!" says Bing.
"Okay," giggles Coco.

Bing steps inside the hoop and spins it around his waist.
"Hulaaaaaa…"

Clatter, clatter

The hoop drops
to the ground
immediately.

"Don't worry, Bing," says Flop. "Try again."
Bing moves forwards and backwards, giggling.
He looks like he's dancing.

"Bing!" giggles Coco.
"It's a *Hula* Hoop, not
a *dancing* hoop!"

"And it's a **jumping hoop!**"
cheers Bing. He puts the hoop
on the ground and jumps in and
out of it.

"Hulas are tricky," Coco tells Bing. "Watch again.

Hu-la, hu-la, hu-la, hu-la!"

As Coco spins the hoop, Bing and Flop count her spins. "One... two... three... four... five... six... seven... EIGHT!"

Clatter, clatter

"Eight!" gasps Coco. "That's my best ever!"
"I'm going to do eight hulas too!" says Bing.

"Here, have another try," suggests Flop. Bing tries again, but the hoop falls straight to the ground.

Clatter, clatter

"It's hard," sighs Bing.
"It used to be hard for me too," explains Coco. "I had to keep trying, and trying, and then ta-dah... I could just hula hula!"

Bing holds the hoop upright. "Look! Charlie can crawl through the hoop!" says Bing. "It's a Charlie-train."

Chooooo-chooooo!

Suddenly, Bing has an idea. "I know! Let's do hulas together, Coco!"

Bing and Coco wriggle and wiggle inside the hoop. It's tricky hard but very fun!

Bing tries spinning it on his own again. He spins the hoop twice and it clatters to the ground. Bing picks it up and spins it again.

"Oh!" says Bing, as the hoop spins round and round.

"I'm doing it!"

"Well done, Bing!" says Flop. "Yes!" cheers Coco.

As Bing picks up the hoop for another try, he gets so excited he starts to spin his whole body around...

"Hu-la, hu-la!"

He spins faster and faster... when suddenly, "Ohhhh..."
He trips on his train and lands on Holly Hula Hoop.

BUMP!

"Oh, are you okay, Bing?" asks Flop.

Bing is okay but the hoop is bent.
"Look what you've done to Holly!" sighs Coco.

She tries to spin the hoop, but it doesn't work. "Oh no, I *loved* Holly Hula!"

"I'm sorry, Coco," says Bing. "I didn't mean to break it."

Flop picks up Holly Hula Hoop and Charlie crawls through it. "Chooooo-choooo!"

"Charlie can still play *tunnel* hoop," says Flop.

"Shall I see if you can still do hoopy *jumping*?" Bing asks Coco.
"Okay," says Coco.
Bing jumps inside the hoop.
"It works! You try it, Coco!"

Jump-a! Jump-a!

"Oh, I can do it really fast!" says Coco, feeling a bit better.

"Why don't we *all* try this?" says Flop, skipping with the hoop.
"You can do it first, Coco," says Bing.
"Good for you, Bing Bunny," says Flop.

Skip-a! Skip-a! Skip-a!

"I did like doing hulas, but I love the *skipping* hoop!" cheers Coco.
"And the *jumping* hoop!" adds Bing.
Charlie giggles.
"Yes, Charlie," says Flop. "And the *tunnel* hoop!"

Hula Hoop... it's a Bing thing.

17

Story quiz

What do you **remember** about the story?

1 **What** was Bing playing with at the start of the story?

 **A**

 **B**

 **C**

2 **Who** came to visit Bing in the story?

 **A**

 **B**

 **C**

3 **Point** to the picture of Holly Hula Hoop.

 **A**

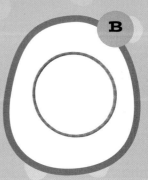 **B**

 **C**

4 **What** other things did Bing, Coco and Charlie use Holly Hula Hoop for?

A Jumping, skipping and as a tunnel

B Digging, throwing and rolling

C Drawing and painting

Answers: 1. C, 2. C, 3. B, 4. A

18

Hula hula!

Bing and Coco are trying to hula with Holly Hula Hoop together!
Can you finish the picture by finding the right jigsaw pieces?

A

B

C

D

E

Answers: A, B, D

Circle spotting

Holly Hula Hoop is a **circle** shape. How many other circle shapes can you spot in this picture? **Point** to each one and count them as you go.

Did you know?
A circle is round. It has **one** line that goes all the way round, and no corners.

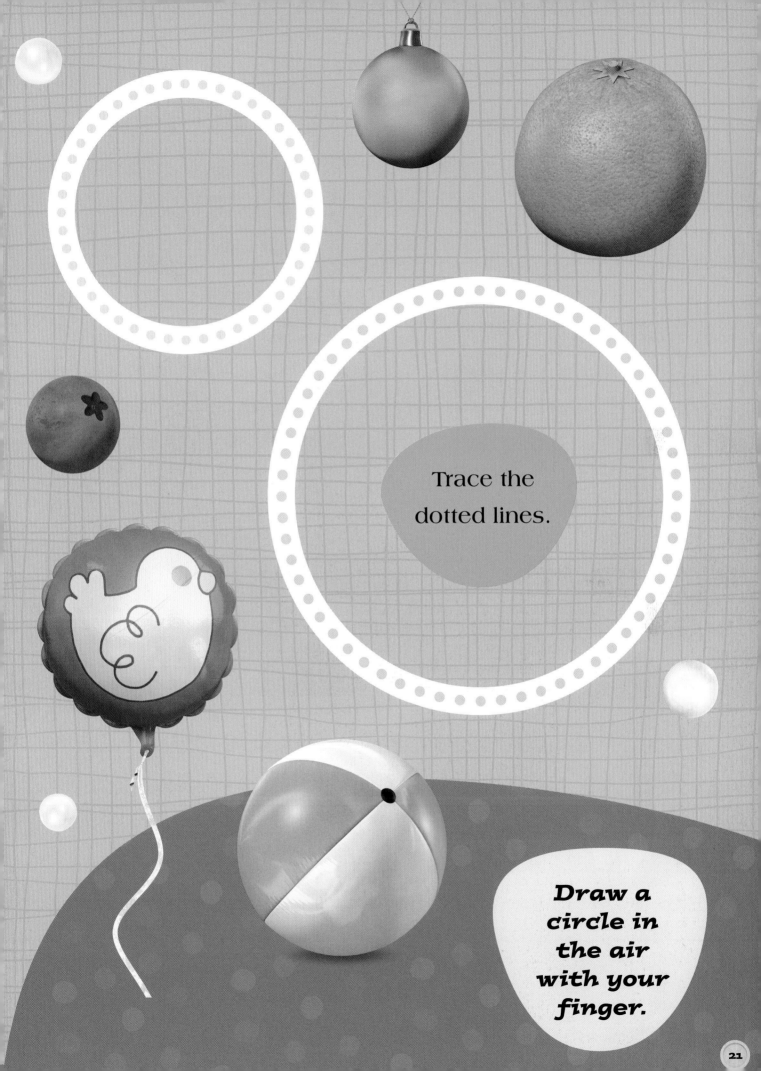

Trace the dotted lines.

Draw a circle in the air with your finger.

Jump up and move game

START

1

2

3

4

5

6

7

8

16

17

18

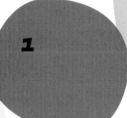

9

10

11

12

15

14

13

FINISH

19

20

How to play:

1. Find someone to play with and each choose a counter.

2. Put both of your counters at the START.

3. Throw the die. Whoever throws the highest number goes first.

4. Take turns to roll the die and move your counters along the board. If you land on a character, jump up and copy their pose. Then move your counter forward one more space.

5. The first player to reach the FINISH is the winner!

Snowy day

Can you help Bing and his friends choose **what to wear** on a cold snowy day? Point to or draw a circle around their **winter clothes**.

 **A**

 **B**

 **C**

 **A**

 **B**

 **C**

 **A**

 **B**

 **C**

Answers: Bing – C, Sula – A, Pando – B

Matching mittens

Bing, Sula and Nicky's gloves are all **mixed up!** Try drawing lines to match the correct **pairs of mittens.**

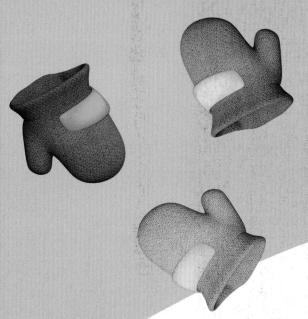

Draw round your hand here. What colour gloves would you like?

Catching snowflakes

Bing, Sula and Pando are wrapped up warm and toasty, ready to catch snowflakes! **Colour in** the picture with your favourite colours.

Big and small

Look at the groups of Christmas presents and help Bing to find the **biggest** one in each group.

Snow patterns

Bing loves playing in the **snow** with his friends.
Draw over the dotty lines to make shapes
and patterns in the snow.

Trace the lines to build **Mr Snowman!**

How many **pebbles** can you count on Mr Snowman? Trace over the number here.

House

Round the corner, not far away,
Bing is making **a house** today...

Bing is using cushions to build a house.

"Need any help, Bing?" asks Flop. "Yes, please," says Bing.

The last cushion is a big one for the roof. Bing shows Flop where to put it. "Thank you, Flop!" says Bing.

Bing sits inside his cushion house. "Come in, Flop!" "Ohh," says Flop. "It's very cosy." The doorbell rings.

DING! DONG!

"I'm going to hide," giggles Bing. He pulls some cushions in front of him and the house and hides behind them.

"Hi, Flop!" says Coco. "Where's Bing?"
"**Bing!**" calls Sula, looking around. "Where are you?"

They walk to the cushion house and Bing
suddenly jumps out.

"BOO!"

"Oh!" gasp Sula and
Coco, giggling.

"I'm in my house!" says Bing.
"Oh, that's like the **Big Bad Wolf** game,"
says Coco. "I love that one!"

"Little Bing, little Bing, can I come in?" asks Sula.
"No, Big Bad Wolf! You can't come in!" laughs Bing.

"Then we'll huff and we'll
puff and we'll

BLOW YOUR HOUSE IN!"

shout Coco and Sula.

Bing comes out of his house and pats it proudly. "You can't blow it in," he says. "This is a *brick* house and it's very, very strong!"

"Let's all play Big Bad Wolf!" suggests Sula. "Can I be the Big Bad Wolf?" asks Bing. He finds a tail in the dressing-up box. "I can wear this," he adds.

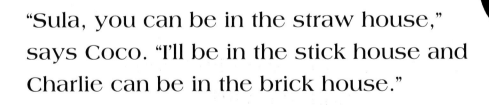

"Sula, you can be in the straw house," says Coco. "I'll be in the stick house and Charlie can be in the brick house."

"And I'm the Big... Bad... Wolf...

Raaar!" shouts Bing.

"You have to be scarier than that, Bing!" says Coco.

"Raaar!"

33

Flop helps Sula make her straw house under the kitchen table.
"Little Sula, little Sula, let me come in!" says Bing.

Sula giggles. "No, Big Bad Wolf. You **can't** come in!"

"Then I'll **huff** and I'll **puff** and I'll **blow** your house in!" shouts Bing.

PFFFFTTTTTT!

Bing chases Sula as she scrambles out from her straw house.

"**Raaar!**"

"The Big Bad Wolf is coming to get me!" says Sula as she giggles and runs away.

Sula races over to Coco. "Help, little Coco! Help!" she says, hiding in Coco's stick house.

Bing comes over. "Little Coco, little Sula, let me come in!"

"No!" giggle Coco and Sula. "Big Bad Wolf, you can't come in!"

"Then I'll **huff** and I'll **puff** and I'll **blow your house in!**" shouts Bing.

PFFFFTTTTTT!

Coco and Sula run over to the brick house and hide with Flop and Charlie.

"Little Charlie, little Coco, little Sula – let me come in!" says Bing.

"No! Big Bad Wolf, you **can't** come in!" say Coco and Sula.

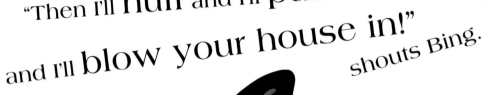

"Then I'll huff and I'll puff and I'll blow your house in!" shouts Bing.

He tries to pull the cushions away to get inside, but he can't.

"Bing!" says Coco, holding the cushions. "It's a *brick* house, remember."

"The wolf can't come into *this* house," explains Sula.

"But I made that house. I want to come in!" says Bing.

Bing throws the top cushion off the house. "I don't want to play any more!"

"But we were just playing the game," explains Sula.

"Sorry," says Bing. "I didn't mean to spoil the game."

"Don't worry, Bing," says Flop.
"It's no big thing. We'll build it again."
They put the cushion back on the house together.

"Raaar!" adds Charlie.

"Now *Charlie* wants to be the **wolf!**" giggles Sula.

Bing puts the wolf tail on Charlie. "Now you're the Big Bad Charlie Wolf!" he giggles.

"Raaaar!" Charlie gurgles.

Building a house...
it's a **Bing thing.**

Story quiz

Can you **remember** what happened in the story?

1 What did Bing use to **build** his house? Point to the right picture.

A
B
C

2 Finish this **sentence:** Bing was the Big Bad _ _ _ _.

A **Frog** B **Wolf** C **Fish**

3 **Point** to what Bing put on from his dressing-up box to play the game.

A
B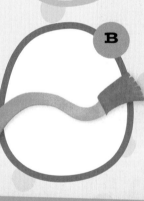
C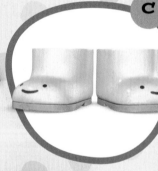

4 Look at the picture and decide which sentence best **describes** it.

A Sula's straw house was **on top of the table.**

B Sula's straw house was **under the table.**

C Sula's straw house was **in the bedroom.**

Answers: 1. A, 2. B, 3. B, 4. B

Who's next?

Bing and his friends are taking it in turns to be the **Big Bad Wolf.** Work out who comes next in each row and draw them in the box...

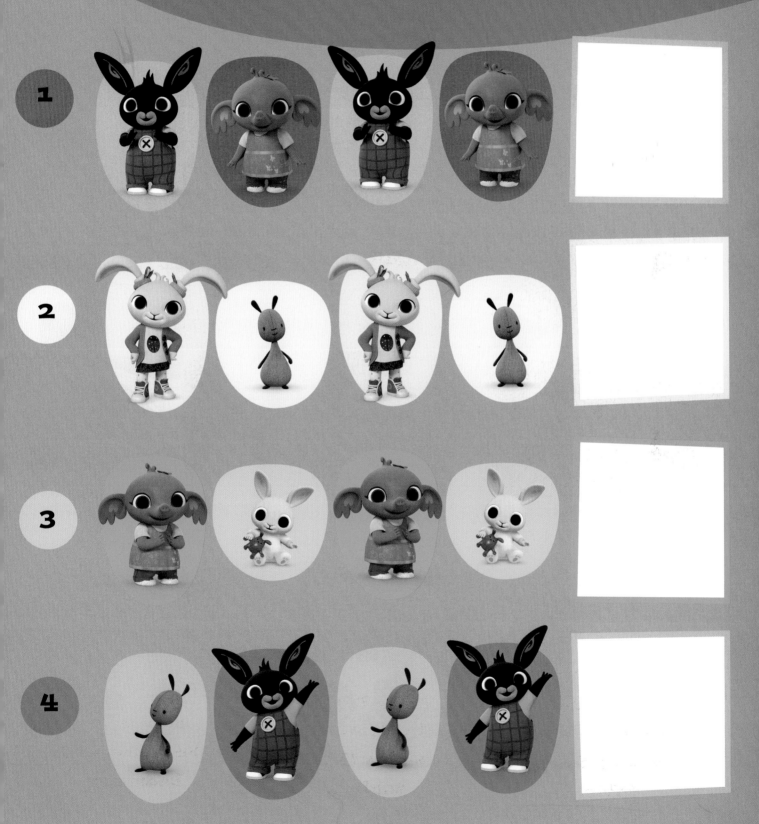

Hide-and-seek

Bing is playing hide-and-seek with Flop, Coco, Sula, Pando and Charlie. It is his turn to seek. Can you help him by **finding** everyone in the big picture?

Colour in each friend as you find them!

Building houses

There are lots of different ways you can build a house like Bing did in the story.

Bing used sofa **cushions** to build his brick house.

Sula used a **table** to make her straw house.

Coco used a **circle of chairs** to make her stick house.

With the help of a grown-up, you could try hanging **blankets** over chairs to make a house.

A grown-up could also help you build a house outside with **sticks**.

Draw a picture of
yourself in your
OWN house below.

Me and my house

By: ....

Odd one out

Bing is helping Flop do a big sort-out.
Can you help them by spotting the
odd one out in each group?

Draw a circle
round the object
that doesn't fit
with the others.

Talkie Taxi!

Bing is **driving** Talkie Taxi. Join the dots and **colour** in the picture with your favourite pencils!

Zoom around the room like you're driving too!

"Vroom vroom!"

Bath time!

Bing is having lots of fun playing with his toys in the **bubbly bath!** Can you spot the **six differences** between the two big pictures?

Colour in a rubber duckie as you spot each difference.

Splish, splash, splosh!

Answers: 1. A rubber duckie is sitting on the bubbles, 2. The bath has changed colour, 3. A purple octopus is sitting on the edge of the bath, 4. Bubble Duck has vanished, 5. The towel has changed colour, 6. A big bubble has popped!

Hop, skip, jump!

Use your finger to help Bing **hop, skip** and **jump** his way along the paving stones to meet his friends at the playground.

Don't tread on any **green** stones!

Can you hop, skip and jump too?

Yummy-delicious festive smoothie

Flop and Bing enjoy making yummy-delicious **smoothies** in Brenda the Blender! Follow these steps to make a **berry festive smoothie.**

You will need:

- a small handful of blueberries (fresh or frozen)
- a small handful of raspberries (fresh or frozen)
- a small handful of strawberries (fresh or frozen)
- half a small banana
- a tablespoon of yoghurt
- a teaspoon of cinnamon
- a teaspoon of honey
- a blender
- cups for serving

Note:
Adjust the amounts to fit your blender and how many servings you need.

Top tip!
If you don't have frozen berries but would like an icy cold smoothie, you can blend some crushed ice into it too.

What to do:
1. Ask a grown-up to help you prepare the ingredients and put them all into a blender.
2. Use the blender to squish up all the ingredients together!
3. Pour your festive smoothie into cups and enjoy!

Stuck

Round the corner, not far away,
Bing is **climbing trees** today...

Bing, Sula, Flop and Amma are playing in the Howly Woods.

"Weeee! Look at me!" shouts Sula from the tyre swing. "Faster, Bing, faster!" Bing gives Sula a big push.

"Weeeeee!"

Bing spots a fallen tree. "Let's climb that flat tree, Sula!" he shouts, running towards it.
"Wait for me, Bing!" says Sula, wriggling out of the tyre.

Bing carefully climbs on to the tree, then puts his arms out to keep his balance.
"Look at me!" he says.
"I'm the **King of the Castle!**"

"I can do that too," says Sula.

Sula tries to climb on to the tree trunk, but it is too high. "I can't get up," she sighs.

Bing shows Sula how he climbed up. "You've got to find a hand-holdy bit and another bit for your foot." "Oh, okay," says Sula.

Sula holds on and pulls herself up. "Yes!" she cheers. **"I'm the Queen of the Castle!"**

Bing shows Sula how he moves along the tree trunk on his tummy. "Bing, you look like a caterpillar!" Sula giggles.

"Now let's go on the **Bouncy Tree!"** says Bing.

Bing and Sula run over to sit on the Bouncy Tree with Flop. "Are you ready?" says Flop.

"Yup!" cheer Bing and Sula together.

Flop bounces the branch up and down.

Boing! Boing! Boing!

"Amma, can you bounce us higher?" asks Sula. "Of course," says Amma.

Amma helps bounce the branch even higher.

Boing! Boing! Boing!

Bing notices a branch higher up. "I want to climb to that tree seat. Can I, Flop?"
"Sure," says Flop.
"Go on up. I'll be right here."

"I'm staying here," says Sula. "I like bouncing best."

Boing! Boing!

Bing climbs up on to the branch. "Wow, look at me!" says Bing. "I'm in the tree seat! Yay!"

Bing spots something in the corner of his eye. "Look, a squirrel!" he gasps. "Hello, Mr Squirrel."

"He's getting acorns. He must be hungry. I'm hungry too," says Sula.
"Well, carroty bagels and hot chocolate are ready when you are," says Amma.

But when Bing tries to get down from the tree seat he can't find a place to put his foot. "Oh," he says, a bit worried. "Are you okay, Bing?" asks Flop.

"Ehm... I'm stuck," says Bing.
"I can't see how to get down."

"It's okay. I'm right here. Just take it slowly. You'll be down in no time," says Flop.
"You just need some help," adds Amma.

"I can help!" offers Sula.

"You have to turn round, Bing," says Sula.
"Good idea, Sula," adds Flop.
"I don't like it," replies Bing. "I can't see."
"I can see, Bing," says Sula. "I can see a foot-stepper."

Sula, Flop and Amma help guide Bing back down.
"That's it," says Flop.

"Now be a **backwards cattypillar** for the last bit," says Sula as Bing shuffles like a caterpillar off the bouncy branch and on to the ground.

"Yay, I did it!" says Bing.
Sula gives Bing a big hug.
"Good for you, Bing Bunny," says Flop.

"I helped Bing climb down!" says Sula.
"Good for you, Sula," says Flop.
"Come on then, caterpillars. Let's eat!"
says Amma.

Bing and Sula race over to the picnic table.
"Oh, hot chocolate! Yum!" says Bing.
"Carroty bagels! Yum!" adds Sula.

Climbing trees...
it's a Bing thing.

Story quiz

Think back to the story.
What can you **remember** about it?

1 What did Sula use as a **swing**? Point to or circle the answer from the story.

 **A**

 **B**

 **C**

2 Colour in the **animal** Bing spotted in the tree.

A

B

C

3 Look at the colours of the **leaves** in this picture from the story. Which season do you think it is?

A *Spring*

B *Summer*

C *Autumn*

D *Winter*

4 Which of these foods did Bing and Sula have in their **picnic**? Point to the right one.

 **A**

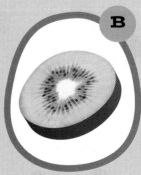 **B**

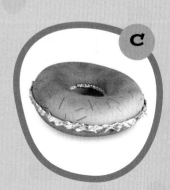 **C**

Answers: 1. A, 2. B, 3. C, 4. C

58

Tree climbing

Bing and Sula had lots of fun playing on the flat tree. Can you spot five differences between these two pictures?

59

Crunchy leaves

Bing loves crunching through autumn leaves. Using your finger or pencil, can you help him get through the leaf maze by only stepping on the yellow leaves?

Start

Finish

60

Hello, Mr Squirrel

Squirrels love eating acorns. Using this picture, colour in the image below of Bing giving Mr Squirrel a tasty snack!

Up and down

Bing climbed up the tree and then came back down. "Up" and "down" are opposites. Can you match these other opposites into pairs?

Cold

Wet

Clean

Happy

Sad

Hot

Dry

Dirty

Point to or draw lines between each pair of opposites.

Christmas stocking

Use this page to colour and decorate your own stocking.

What would you like to find in your stocking this Christmas?

Christmas lantern

Follow the simple steps to make
a paper lantern just like Bing's!

You will need:

- an A4 piece of thin card
- a pencil
- a ruler
- pens, paints or stickers for decoration
- safety scissors
- a rubber
- tape

What to do:

1 Turn your card lengthways and draw a vertical line 2cm from each end.

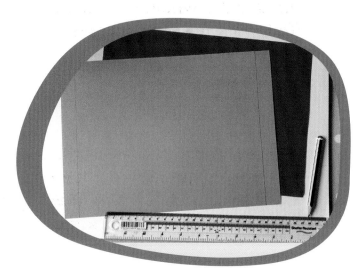

2 Ask an adult to help you cut along the lines. Keep one strip to turn into a handle for your Christmas lantern.

3 Fold the piece of card in half lengthways. Draw a guideline 2cm from the edge of the folded side.

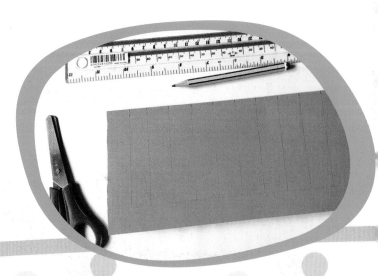

4 Use a ruler to draw vertical lines 2cm apart along the strip, stopping where you have drawn the guideline.

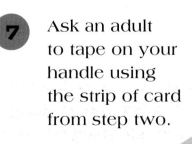

5 Ask an adult to help you cut along the lines to make fringes the whole way along. Rub out the guideline and decorate the lantern.

6 Roll the card into a cylinder shape and ask an adult to help you tape it together at the top and the bottom.

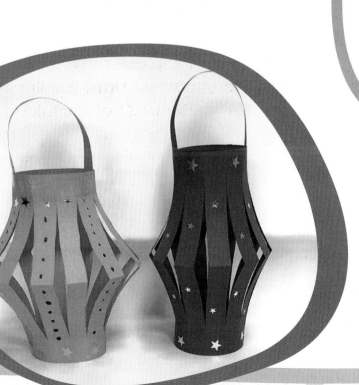

7 Ask an adult to tape on your handle using the strip of card from step two.

Bing's seasons

Bing has fun with his friends all through the year!
Tick the season that matches the picture.

1

A Autumn

B Spring

2

A Spring

B Winter

3

A Summer

B Winter

4

A Autumn

B Spring

Answers: 1. A, 2. B, 3. A, 4. B

66

A Christmas wish

Bing really wants a Hoppity Rocket Sledge this Christmas.

Do you have a special Christmas wish? Draw it here.

When you have finished drawing, trace over the letters below.

Merry Christmas!

It's . . . Christmas!

Can you spot all the festive items in the big picture of Bing and his friends on Christmas Day?

Tick off each item when you spot it.